D0354355

The Swan's Child

by SJOERD KUYPER

illustrated by Jan Jutte

translated by Patricia Crampton

Holiday House / *New York*

This translation has been made possible with the financial support of the Foundation for the Production and Translation of Dutch Literature.
First published in The Netherlands in three separate volumes (*Josje* 1989, *Josje's Droom* 1992, *Josje's Lied* 1999) by Uitgeverij Leopold, Amsterdam
First published in English in Great Britain under the title *Josie* in 2000 by Mammoth, an imprint of Egmont Children's Books Limited, a division of Egmont Holding Limited, 239 Kensington High Street, London W8 6SA
First published in the United States by Holiday House, Inc. in 2006

Library of Congress Cataloging-in-Publication Data
Kuyper, Sjoerd.
[Josie]
The swan's child / Sjoerd Kuyper ; translated by Patricia Crampton;
illustrated by Jan Jutte.
p. cm.
Previously published in English under the title: Josie. London : Mammoth, 2000.
Summary: After Josie's soldier husband is killed in battle, the animals who inhabit her magical world help her cope with grief by locking away her sorrows.
ISBN 0-8234-1861-8
[1. Fantasy.] I. Crampton, Patricia. II. Jutte, Jan, ill. III. Title.
PZ7.K9718Sw 2005
[Fic]—dc22
2004058482

ISBN-13: 978-0-8234-1861-9
ISBN-10: 0-8234-1861-8

This book is dedicated to Margje, my wife, with all my love.

Josie's Song, the third story, is written in memory of Anne Holm, who wrote *Peter*, the most beautiful book I have ever read. It ends with the line: 'There was something that he could never forget – that the good in all of us always lives on and that even consciousness never disappears completely . . . that death does not exist.'

Contents

Book One

JOSIE

One

Like a great white ship, the swan sailed into the little harbour. On her back sat a baby. It made a pretty picture, the naked child on the ship of white feathers. The child's little arms were clasped round the swan's neck, and it sat warmly between the great wings.

The animals from the little harbour town ran out of their houses to the quay. They made encouraging noises, but the swan came no closer. She drifted quite silently in the middle of the harbour. The baby cried.

The animals ran back to their houses, and reappeared with bread and sponge fingers, rusks and bananas. The pig brought a bottle of milk. They stood in a row on the quay, making their encouraging noises. But the swan came no closer.

Let's go, then, thought the pig. He tossed the bottle in a great arc into the water, just beside the swan. The other animals followed his example.

You could see that the swan knew what was good for the baby. First she swam up to the bread, then to the bottle of milk and to a banana. The rest she ate herself. When there was nothing left, the baby let go of the swan's neck and tumbled over backwards among the feathers. The swan laid her beak against the baby's cheek.

The animals on the quay whispered softly, the sea rocked the harbour, the child and the swan fell asleep.

'We must catch them!' the kingfisher told the pig.
'It can't work, can it – a swan and a baby?'

But the pig thought it could.

'As long as we feed them well,' he said.

And so they did.

Every day the animals from the little harbour
town threw milk and bread and bananas to the child,
and rusks and sponge biscuits to the swan. Every day
the baby grew fatter. The swan sank lower and lower
in the water. But she did not come any closer to the
quay.

The pig thought: Who is this child? And who is the swan? Can they understand each other? Are they related? Where do they come from?

'The child is getting too heavy!' the kingfisher told the pig. 'Only the swan's head is still above water. And a little bit of neck . . .'

'But the baby loves it,' said the pig. 'You can see that, in every way.'

It was true. The water was already above its navel, but the child splashed it with flat palms and crowed and trampled, and look at that . . . the trampling helped!

One day the swan was lying so still and deep in the water that she could no longer move. The animals from the little harbour town held their breath.

But . . . the baby trampled its little legs and used its hands as oars. It swept them through the water: one by one, from front to back, left right, left right, and there . . . they moved slowly forward. The child steered the swan towards the quay.

There were steps there, stone steps from the bottom of the sea up to the high quay. The child steered the swan towards the steps. The swan's breast came to rest on the step just under the water. The child set its little feet on the step, left right, beside the swan, and stood up.

It stood up!

And that was when everyone saw that it was a little girl.

She walked up the steps. She walked! With legs bowed from sitting on the swan all the time, but she walked. She climbed! The pig took her in his arms and walked off the quay, away from the harbour. The little girl did not look round.

The swan shook out her feathers and swam into the harbour, away from the steps, out of the harbour, away from the child. She did not look round.

But when she was sailing on the sea like a great white ship, that was when she stretched her neck, lifted her head to the sky and sang.

The pig took the child home with him and dressed her in a lovely little white dress made of lace. He picked her up and carried her to the looking-glass. Together they looked at the pig and the little girl in the glass. The little girl said:

'Swan.'

But the pig called her Josie.

Two

The pig was an old carpenter.

His name was Alexander and he lived in a big house on the edge of the little town. Next to the house was the stable with the carriage in it, and next to that a smaller house. That was where Cousin Donkey lived. Cousin Donkey pulled the carriage when he had to. When he didn't, he polished the brasswork and rubbed grease into the leather reins.

The houses, the carriage and the stable were made of wood; the carpenter had built them himself. Anything that can be made of wood, he made: wardrobes, chairs, beds, pot-racks, tables, straight flagpoles . . . Everything the old carpenter made was wonderful. He made furniture for all the animals in the little harbour town. Cousin Donkey delivered it. In this way they earned good money. Yes, they were rich.

Then Josie came to the big house.

And everything changed.

The old carpenter stood in his workshop and looked around. His hand stroked the smooth back of a chair. He could easily make another chair just like it. Easily done. Just as beautiful, perhaps even more so. But more beautiful than Josie? Impossible.

His hand stroked the top of a table. A table like this, he thought, I can make twenty times over. Each one more beautiful than the last. But more beautiful than Josie? No . . . Beds, wardrobes, chairs? They would be wonderful, certainly! But not as beautiful as Josie.

The carpenter locked the door of his workshop. He went outside, because Josie was playing there – so beautiful. She was wearing her white dress. He pinched his arm to find out if he was dreaming. He pinched hard, it hurt, and the carpenter smiled. He was wide awake. Josie called him Sanders.

One year later Sanders opened the door to his workshop again. He chose a big wardrobe and took out the drawers. He unscrewed the doors. He tapped gently with his hammer against the sides and caught them in his arms as they fell. Then all that was left of the wardrobe

was a pile of wood. Wonderful wood, smooth and shining. From the wood he made a doll's house for Josie.

Sanders did not know where Josie had been born, or what egg she had crept out of. For even that was possible . . . It must have been in the spring, he was sure of that. Another spring floated palely green among the branches of the chestnut tree behind his house. So tomorrow would be Josie's birthday.

The doll's house was exactly like Sanders' own big wooden house. Much smaller, of course, but everything was there: the rooms, the kitchen, the attic, and the

11

workshop, too. It was locked. But if you lay on your stomach you could look in through the window and see tiny wardrobes, tables, beds, chairs and pot-racks as small as the letters on postage stamps.

There were also two dolls in the house. One looked just like Josie. She was wearing a white dress and playing with a teeny-weeny doll's house standing in the main room of the doll's house. The other doll looked exactly like Sanders. He was sitting on a chair, watching the doll that looked like Josie.

For a whole year Josie played with the doll's house every day. The white dress was getting too small for her.

Old Sanders carefully took his carriage to pieces. Out of the wood, brasswork and leather he made a little carriage. He made a stable too. There was a doll that looked exactly like Cousin Donkey. He was standing in the stable polishing the brass.

After another year Sanders made Josie a wonderful, wooden swan, but that she would not play with.

'Swans are not made of wood,' she said.

But she was not angry.

When she was five Sanders bought Josie the first part of a book that had everything in it. He taught her to read.

In the summer they sat under the chestnut tree and

in the autumn they were still sitting there. It was a long time since Sanders had made any furniture for the animals of the little harbour town. His money was running out. But it didn't matter, he said, and Josie didn't mind either. You can still cook delicious dishes with quite cheap ingredients: cabbage and beans and potatoes. And so she grew and grew, and the carpenter grew older.

With the last of his money Sanders bought a thin sheet of silver and two thin sheets of gold. All for Josie, he thought, and he made a mouth-organ for her. He made the bottom and the top of gold and with the silver he made the little tongues inside, which sing the songs when you blow into the right holes.

Josie learned to play it in the spring. In the summer she could already play sad songs such as 'Old Black Joe', and in the autumn she also knew the jollier tunes you can dance to.

They were sitting under the chestnut tree, Josie and Sanders. What a pity the carpenter was so old that he could no longer dance.

'Oh, lass,' he said, 'how I used to dance!'

So he made her a pair of glasses for looking at the past. He made the glasses out of three chestnut leaf stalks and told Josie to put them on her nose. Josie did.

'Now shut your eyes tight,' said Sanders.

Josie did, and Sanders did the same. He had put on a pair of glasses too.

'Eyes shut, and just look,' he said. 'Then you'll see the past. Can you see how I danced, back then . . .?'

But Josie couldn't see.

'Oh no, of course not,' said Sanders. 'With these glasses you can only see your own past – what a shame.'

'I see,' said Josie, her eyes shut so tightly that the glasses were quite lopsided. 'I see a swan coming into the little harbour like a great white ship.'

'Yes, I see it,' said Sanders, for that was his past, too.

'Look, look!' cried Josie happily. 'There's a baby sitting on her back!'

Then came the year when Josie was seven.

Old Sanders opened the door to his workshop and went in. He was troubled: he did not know what to make for Josie this year. The workshop was almost empty. All that was left was one wardrobe, one flagpole, one bed, one table and one chair. Against the wall hung one pot-rack.

It was winter, and spring was a long way off. The little harbour was frozen over and the roofs of the houses bowed under the weight of snow. Sanders had plenty of time to make something really beautiful, if only he knew what . . .

At that moment a chill winter breeze blew open the window on to the garden and a bare branch of the chestnut tree thrust its way in. The carpenter decided to make a tree, a tree to stand by the doll's house. The chestnut tree.

He smiled and began to break up his last pieces of furniture. He needed a lot of wood. Not only for the trunk and the branches, but also for the thin twigs on the branches and the thick roots below the trunk. It was to be a tree with leaves and pink flowers in the spring.

Sanders knew that he would have to make the tree outside, so that all the time he was working, he would be able to see how the tree itself had done it. Now, while it was still winter, and the branches were bare, he could see everything clearly. He must be finished before the spring.

He picked up his beams, planks, laths and battens and pushed them out through the window. He arranged the wood under the chestnut tree and looked up at the trunk. The tree was taller than the house, so the toy tree must also be much taller than the doll's house. But how much taller? Twice as tall? Three times? Ten metres taller, eleven, or seventeen?

The old carpenter climbed up the branches to measure the tree. He climbed to the very top. He looked down. Far below him he saw his house. The windows were lit and he could see into the big room.

There was Josie, standing by her doll's house. She looked out and saw Sanders, high up in the tree. She waved to him with both arms, like branches waving in the wind.

Then the carpenter knew that the tree must be as tall as Josie. Just as tall, because that would suit the doll's house perfectly. As tall as Josie! And every year, as Josie grew some more, he would make the tree taller, so that it would always be as tall as Josie.

And perhaps, thought the carpenter, and only *perhaps*, if I make good roots, roots like thin reeds that can suck water from the depths of the earth, then perhaps . . . the tree will grow! Grow, like a child – then it will grow along with Josie!

Sanders smiled down at Josie and waved back. With both arms – he was so happy. Everything for Josie, he thought again. Then he fell and Josie saw him falling. He fell, reached the ground and broke his neck. Then he was dead.

Josie ran to Cousin Donkey.

'Sanders is dead!' she cried.

'Dead?' asked Cousin Donkey. 'What's that, then?'

Josie knew the answer, but she didn't know how to put it. Not very well, anyway.

'Dead,' said Josie. 'That is . . . never more.'

'Never more what?' asked Cousin Donkey.

'Never more everything,' said Josie.

'Everything never more,' Cousin Donkey nodded.

'That's dead,' said Josie.

They were silent, they thought about it, they didn't cry.

'And you have to cry,' said Josie, 'because you're thinking about something nice and the nice thing has been done by someone who's dead. Or something kind . . . Someone who made wonderful things for you. Out of wood . . .'

'Sanders,' said Cousin Donkey.

'Sanders is dead,' said Josie.

Cousin Donkey went with her to look. Then he saw it too. The old carpenter was lying in the snow under the chestnut tree. His smile was still warm.

The animals from the little harbour town came along – all of them. They called Sanders a lovely death. Josie could not understand what was lovely about death.

The animals made a coffin. Not a beautiful one, because only Sanders could do that. But a strong one. They buried Sanders in the place where they had found him: under the chestnut tree, under the snow, in the hard ground. On his grave they set a big stone and on the stone were the words:

Alexander went away,
And he took his smile along.
Nowhere need he ever fear,
Nor be lonely anywhere,
For he took his smile along.

That was a poem. Cousin Donkey had made it up and it made Josie cry so much, so dreadfully, that the kingfisher said: 'All right, then. You just come along home with me. I'll spoil you, then the grief will wear off.'

He put an arm round her shoulders and led her away. Cousin Donkey stayed with the house and the stable to watch over the house and the stable and the grave.

The kingfisher would not let Josie cry in bed.

'You can stay as long as you like,' said the kingfisher, 'and welcome. But you do your crying over the washbasin.'

Above the washbasin hung a mirror, with Josie's face in it, so she stopped crying, but her grief didn't wear off until she dared to go back to Sanders' big wooden house, to the stable and the grave.

Spring was already far advanced. Cousin Donkey sat on the step in front of the stable in the sunshine, and behind the house the chestnut tree was in flower. Josie saw the tree's thousands of flowers, the big hands that held the pink flower candles fast – as if in a procession round the trunk. She went into the house.

She walked through the rooms, which were so empty without Sanders. She went into the workshop – *so* empty. She could no longer live here.

A spring breeze blew open the window on to the garden. One branch of the chestnut tree leaned cheekily inside. Josie pushed the branch aside and looked out of the window.

The pink petals of the chestnut tree fell on the white petals of a hawthorn tree standing nearby. The white petals were already brown at the edges, the spring was so far advanced. And the pink fell so beautifully on the old white – so splendidly that Josie thought: the white is death, the pink is our comfort . . .

Then she almost understood why it was a good thing that animals and people die. Almost. It really mattered very little . . . She climbed out of the window.

There stood the tree. Josie hoisted herself on to the lowest branch and climbed upwards from there, to the spot where Sanders had been standing when he waved . . . So she was climbing higher than she had ever been in her life, oh, far higher than the house, she climbed. Twice as high? Three times? Ten metres, eleven, seventeen? She climbed right to the top.

It was there that she built herself a tree-house. A

house of her own! The tree-house looked just like Sanders' house, and like the doll's house, of course. Bigger than the doll's house, smaller than the house, exactly between the two, and as long as you didn't think about big or small, exactly the same.

There she read the first part of the book which had everything in it. She grew, and the tree grew too. She read the book for seven long years, and when she had finished it, she shut it.

She looked up and saw the soldier.

Three

Once upon a time there was a soldier, but there was no war.

The soldier had a cannon, one cannon, and a cannonball, one cannonball. He had no house, he had a room, one room. The cannon was as big as the room. The soldier slept in his cannon, the cannonball was his pillow.

The ball was so hard that the soldier dreamed of a gap in a wall. Through the gap he saw the sea, and on its waves floated a ship. It was a beautiful dream.

Someone knocked on the door. Josie brought in the newspaper. Josie cared about the soldier, but the soldier didn't care about her; he didn't even see her standing there. He took the paper and read:

The soldier was furious! Still no war! He turned round and polished the cannon and the cannonball until the war should arrive. But the war did not come. Only Josie came, every evening, with the paper.

And so it went on, for many years. Then Josie snipped three hairs from her head. She put them under the soldier's doormat – then she knew what he was dreaming.

The next morning a swan came to the soldier's window. The bird threw her wings wide and cried:

'War! It's war! The Tar Men are coming to get you!' The soldier's heart leaped for joy.

'Is it really true?' he asked.

But the swan had vanished. There was a knock at the door. The soldier opened it. There stood three men, in clothes as black as night. They were called Tar, all three of them – they were so much alike. The men carried the cannon down the stairs. The soldier carried the cannonball himself.

'Go down to the harbour,' said the men. 'There's a ship there, the enemy ship. Fire!'

The soldier went down to the little harbour. On the water floated a great white ship. The soldier fired. Bull's-eye. The tall mast broke and fell down on the ship.

'Bull's-eye!' cried the soldier.

He turned his head proudly, but the Tar Men had vanished. The ship had vanished, too, and the animals stayed indoors. Scared. The soldier stood on the quayside, all alone.

He went back to his house and dragged his cannon up the stairs. He wanted to sleep, he was tired, but he had no cannonball now! He took off his soldier's uniform and folded it into a pillow.

The clothes were so soft that the soldier dreamed of a window in the morning. It stood open. In the window sat a swan with a broken wing. The soldier woke up crying.

Every night the soldier dreamed about the swan. He thought: I will make the bird better. He wanted to catch her, but the swan stumbled quickly away. But the soldier knew that a dream would come when the bird would let herself be caught. *Then* I'll make her better!

So he started sleeping by day as well.

And the dream came. It was a beautiful dream: the bird let herself be caught and the soldier took her in his arms. He placed a stick beside her wing and wound a bandage round it. The swan stumbled away from him, but look . . .!

One dream later the swan came flying in on strong wings. She threw her wings round the soldier's neck and the soldier woke up in the arms of the newspaper girl.

'Were *you* the swan?' asked the soldier.

'I was the swan,' she said. 'I was the swan, the men and the ship. My name is Josie.'

But the soldier named her Swan.

Book Two

JOSIE'S
DREAM

Four

A black ship glided over the sea. It was night-time. The sky was as black as the ship, because wherever the ship sailed, the stars blew out their lanterns. The moon hid her face, and the sea was as black as the sky. On the ship's afterdeck stood three men, with black clothes and chalk-white faces. Their mouths were moving, all three mouths at exactly the same time. It looked as if they were singing, but there was no sound.

'The Tar Men,' whispered Josie. 'They are sailing through my dream. Oh, don't let them come near me again!'

She opened her eyes and dried her tears on her pyjamas. Running to the window she looked out over

the little town that lay at the foot of the hill. She saw the town and the harbour and the empty sea.

The little harbour was like a painting, the houses reflected, motionless, in the water, which lay smooth as glass against the quay. The houses and the quay had been so brightly cleaned and scrubbed and polished yesterday for the feast that the painting looked brand new. Just done. With paint that was still wet . . . High above the sea stood the moon, fine as a baby's fingernail. The sun came up, and between sun and moon the bell began to ring.

The animals from the little harbour ran out of their houses to the quay. They carried mirrors and beautiful things made of cut glass, Christmas tree baubles and silver stars, nail scissors and boxes full of medals. If it shone it would do. But before they went to work they kissed each other. Carefully. Many things were breakable.

'One kiss for Josie, one for her soldier.'

The kingfisher did not join in. He stood at his front

door, looking at the paper in his wing. He was muttering the words he had written on it. No one must be allowed to hear them, they were still secret. It was a speech, a speech for Josie and for her soldier. He read and read . . . The words were so beautiful, the kingfisher thought.

The other animals climbed on to steps, windowsills and rooftops. They threw ropes to each other and made them fast on chimneys and flagpoles. They cheered like sailors on the highest yard. On the ropes they hung the mirrors and stars and baubles and scissors, the medals and the beautiful things made of cut glass. The moon vanished behind the blue sky, the sun spread its light over the little harbour and everything that was hanging on the ropes reflected the light.

'Twinkling light,' said the duck.

'Dancing light,' said the sheep.

'Dancing like kangaroos,' said the kangaroo.

'Like firework kangaroos,' said the young buffalo. And the kangaroo nodded.

The bell rang on and on. The badger was the captain of the bell-tower and he himself took charge of the bell rope. He pulled the rope and the rope pulled the great bronze bell high in the tower and the great bronze bell high in the tower pulled back on the rope and the rope pulled back on the badger and so again and again the badger found himself hanging in the air, his legs thrashing. Up in the tower the bell swung more and more wildly to and fro. Anyone in the wide world who did not hear the bell must have been deaf.

Everything was ready for the feast. The young buffalo blew his trumpet and the sound rang through the early morning.

And look!

The door of the big wooden house on the hill at the edge of the little town swung open, and on the threshold stood Josie. At the same moment a beautiful bridal coach rode out. The soldier was sitting on the box and Cousin Donkey walked between the smooth wooden shafts.

'Swan!' cried the soldier.

He called Josie 'Swan', but the animals thought that was ridiculous. They called Josie 'Josie'.

'Swan!' the soldier cried again.

He ran to Josie, picked her up and carried her to the coach. He put her on the box. Cousin Donkey began to pull. The soldier had just time to jump up beside Josie on the box, Cousin Donkey was making such speed. He pulled, and as he pulled he sang a song. He had made it up himself. It was a wedding song.

The ride from the house to the quay was quite

short, but the song was a long one, and Cousin Donkey trotted eight times through all the streets and alleys of the little town so that he could sing all the couplets. The coach rocked wildly to and fro as Cousin Donkey ran, singing and springing crazily between the shafts. Josie and her soldier almost fell off the coach, but fortunately they too were rocking, with laughter, so they reached the little harbour safely after all.

The animals were standing there cheering.

But they must be quiet at once, said the kingfisher, because he was going to make his speech.

'Josie,' announced the kingfisher.

But then he began to cry so heartbreakingly that he could not read any more. Josie jumped down from the coach and ran over to him.

'That was wonderful,' she said. She kissed the kingfisher on the wet orange feathers right under his eyes. 'Come,' she said, 'we are going to enjoy ourselves.'

The young buffalo blew his trumpet again, and so began the most beautiful wedding feast ever celebrated.

First there was a procession.

The animals had made four wagons, carrying everything they knew about Josie and her soldier. The wagons were decorated green and brown with seaweed, scraped yesterday from the wooden posts of the quay, and in the seaweed gleamed black and mother-of-pearl mussel shells.

On the first wagon Josie was entering the little harbour on the back of a swan; on the second wagon Josie was sitting next to old Sanders under the chestnut tree; on the third wagon the soldier lay waiting in his cannon for war to come, and on the last wagon stood a big cake of green and brown and black and mother-of-pearl, and on top of it stood Josie and her soldier – the bridal pair.

After that came the presents.

Josie was given part two of the book with everything in it by the soldier. She gave the soldier nothing because to do so would not have been proper. But she loved him, so much that 'soldier' was no longer a word to her but a name, a beloved name. The animals carried in armloads of presents. The kingfisher gave two big umbrellas. One for Josie, one for the soldier.

'One would have been enough,' laughed Josie. 'We're married now, aren't we?'

'You are sure to have a quarrel,' said the kingfisher. 'Just as it's raining . . . You'll see.'

Then the game began.

The animals ran to their houses to fetch their hoops and the swallow perched on the bell-tower. When the animals came out again the swallow dived from the tower to the quay and flitted and swerved and zigzagged to and fro just above the heads of the animals. The trick was to make the swallow fly through your hoop. It took a long time. With peals of laughter the bird flew left and right past all the hoops, and just as you were thinking: *now* I've got her, you hadn't. Sometimes you fell into the harbour, but that wasn't bad. A dolphin would fish you out and you could ride on his back, and then you had a chance. Because, oh, how the swallow laughed when you fell into the water! She flopped limply through the air and then if you held up your hoop, yes, then you had her!

When the game had lasted long enough, Josie and the soldier held up their hoops together in a big figure of eight. The swallow streaked down to the very spot where the hoops touched in the middle. The game was over.

The kangaroo had won again.

'Great party,' said the kangaroo.

'A bit dark,' said the duck.

'Let's get the torches,' said the sheep.

'The fireworks!' cried the buffalo.

'Wireferks!' cried Cousin Donkey, who had been dipping deeply into the wine. 'Tight up the lorches! Hopla . . .' He turned the wedding coach round.

'Choke!' he cried. 'Choke!' He crawled underneath the coach and fell asleep.

The soldier took Josie in his arms and carried her to the house on the hill. They spent a long time standing side by side at the window, watching the party down by the little harbour. The rockets split open high above the empty sea in a thousand festoons of brilliantly coloured stars.

'Come,' said Josie.

She took her soldier by the hand and when they lay embracing in the big bed they could still hear the fireworks.

Later Josie dreamed. She saw the fireworks returning to earth, falling from the sky: glowing spheres, falling stars, streaked through her dream. The fireworks were falling! Not into the little harbour, no, on to cannons on a black ship sailing over a black sea, under a black sky . . .

On the afterdeck of the ship stood the Tar Men. Their mouths were moving, all three mouths exactly together. They were singing. Josie understood the words one by one and all together: they were singing songs of war and parting. The Tar Men were on their way to her again! Their hands pointed into the distance, and there, under the night sky, lay the little harbour.

Josie and her soldier slept late into the day. They could do that because the badger left the bell in peace.

40

Everyone needed their sleep. In fact, the bell had been rung so often during the wedding that it could do without ringing for a day.

Five

The big wooden house on the hill had been standing empty for a long time. It had been built by Sanders, the old carpenter, and that was why it was so fine. First Sanders lived there alone and then when Josie came they lived there together. But Sanders died and the house was suddenly so empty that Josie was frightened. She was still young.

But if you marry a soldier you are no longer afraid. Of nothing and no one, no one at all. They had dusted, swept and painted, they had beaten carpets and hung doors straight. The animals all helped and after a week they had finished. Now Josie dared to live in the house again, with her soldier. And Cousin Donkey – who had kept watch for years over house and garden and stable – Cousin Donkey was content.

'But,' he said, 'whoever lives here, it is and always will be Sanders' house.'

Josie took her bits and pieces into the house and the soldier brought his cannon. They pushed it down the stairs, to the cellar. They put the cannon behind boxes full of white dresses – it looked as if they were hiding it. Finally they dragged the bed up the stairs, to the room with the high windows overlooking the harbour.

In the silence of the morning after the wedding all the animals were still in bed. They slept deeply. Their windows were open and they dreamed of open windows, of shiny things on ropes which they themselves had tied, of waves making their way into the little harbour, of wind in their fur. And what they dreamed was the truth, but they did not know that. They were asleep.

Josie was the only one who dreamed of the black ship mooring at the quay. She saw the Tar Men coming ashore in the bright morning light, she heard their footsteps in the streets and alleyways, she saw their shadows passing by houses and doors. The shadows were so black; when they fell across things, the things did not turn grey, but became invisible, as if covered with a cloth.

Josie was the only one who saw them coming. And that was how it happened that the men did not even have to knock when they stood before Sanders' house. Josie had already opened the door.

'It's you,' she said.

The Tar Men said nothing. They did not even nod. They were they. That was enough. They brought a letter for the soldier.

'A letter from the king!' cried the soldier. 'To congratulate us. How kind . . .'

Josie shook her head.

'It's war,' she said.

And so it was. The letter said:

It's war. Take your cannon and go on board.

The soldier looked about him, as if he wanted to escape.

'Swan,' he said softly.

The Tar Men were standing in the bedroom doorway.

'Get your cannon.'

'I don't know where it is,' said the soldier.

'In the cellar, behind boxes full of white dresses.'

'It's so heavy,' said the soldier.

'We will pull it.'

'I have no cannonball,' said the soldier.

'We have cannonballs.'

'The cannon is old now,' said the soldier. 'Perhaps it can't shoot any longer.'

'Cannons never shoot,' said the Tar Men. 'It's always men who shoot.'

Josie gave her soldier a mouth-organ. At the wedding she could not give him anything. It was not done. Now she could. The bottom and the top of the mouth-organ were made of gold and the little tongues inside, that sing the songs when you blow into the right gaps, were made of silver. She had been given it by Sanders when she was six years old.

'Play it when you are tired in the evenings,' she said.

The animals had come out of their houses and stood blank-faced on the quay, watching the soldier go on board. On the ship stood a bed with black sheets on it, and even a black blanket.

'Lie down,' said the Tar Men. 'You are tired and soon you will have to fight.'

'I am not tired,' said the soldier.

He stood proudly on the deck. He fought against his tears and he won. He filled his chest with air; he did not cry. He stood proudly on the deck and looked at Josie.

'Swan!' he cried.

He swayed.

'You are tired,' said the Tar Men.

And they laid hands on him. They held him fast and pushed him towards the bed. Tiredness poured from their fingers into the soldier's body.

'You are tired, *so* tired,' they said.

And the soldier had never been *so* tired before. He fought against sleep and he lost. The Tar Men spread the sheets and the blanket over him. Only the soldier's head could be seen on the black pillow – white as a letter that you read and reread in the night.

The ship sailed away, out of the little harbour, and even the animals had gloomy thoughts. But to Josie they said:

'He will be back. Your soldier will come back. He will be back, we know that for certain. Depend on it, he will come back, your soldier.'

And Josie nodded.

She looked at the black ship, which was now sailing on the sea with her soldier on board, her sleeping soldier, carrying in his knapsack the silver and gold harmonica, and she knew what he was dreaming, and she thought, someone who dreams like that does not come back.

Cousin Donkey came to stand beside her. His eyes were streaming, but that was probably because of the wine.

'I'll take you for one more ride,' he said.

He put the coach back on its wheels and stood between the smooth shafts. Josie climbed up on the box.

'Kind of you,' she said.

'One more time . . . because it is such a sorrowful day,' said Cousin Donkey. 'But it must not become a habit.'

He began to pull. Slowly he walked through the narrow streets of the little town. Josie sat on the box and saw what her soldier was dreaming. Softly she sang it aloud.

'What a sorrowful song,' said Cousin Donkey. 'You still have me!'

'That's why I sing it,' said Josie, 'to hear you say that.'

She began to sing again.

'Now you're singing it *again*!'

'Because I wanted you to say it *again*.'

'What?'

'That I still have you.'

'Well, once more, then,' said Cousin Donkey. 'But it must not become a habit: you still have me . . .'

Josie began to sing her song again.

'Hey there,' said Cousin Donkey, 'are you going to go on singing that for ever?'

'I want to hear you say it for ever,' said Josie. 'That I still have you . . .'

Cousin Donkey turned round between the shafts of the coach and looked Josie straight in the eyes.

'You still have me,' he said. 'You still have me . . .'

He began to walk backwards:

'You still have me . . .'

Thus he pulled the coach through the alleys of the little town.

'You still have me . . .'

Josie began to sing again, and after each line of her song Cousin Donkey said:

'You still have me . . .'

It made a lovely harmony.

Six

But of course Josie did not only have Cousin Donkey. When she came home to Sanders' big house all the animals were waiting there, to comfort her. Only the kingfisher stood outside, on the look-out.

'It's necessary,' he said. 'It's important for someone to be on the look-out. It's very important. That's why I'm doing it.'

He shaded his eyes with his wing and peered out.

Josie went into the house. The young buffalo blew his trumpet. The strident tones flew up along the walls and the windows jingled. The animals had formed a club, he said, the Josie Club, and he, the buffalo, was the boss. He read out the rules:

1. Do what the boss says.

2. Don't cry too easily.

3. Don't break any furniture.

4. Keep a look-out.

5. Comfort Josie.

'Comfort!' cried the buffalo.

'Comfort!' cried the other animals.

And they winked at Josie, because the boss said they should.

Josie thought it was very sweet, but she so much wanted to be quite alone. Just for a moment.

'No one who is sad should be alone,' said the buffalo. 'We're not going away until your soldier has come back.'

'Comfort!' cried the animals, winking.

If only I can be alone in the evening, thought Josie. In the evening my soldier will be tired from fighting. He will be lying on his camp-bed, playing his harmonica. Then I shall hear his music and see what he's thinking.

'Play,' she whispered softly, 'play when you're alone . . . then I shall be close to you.'

'What did you say?' cried the animals.

'Nothing,' said Josie, 'I said nothing.'

'Comfort!' cried the buffalo.

'Comfort!' cried the animals.

The day lasted a long time. The sun crept across the sky like a tortoise and the soldier did not play his harmonica. At least, Josie heard nothing. Perfectly sensible, she thought. Don't play and don't think, there among the cannons. This evening I shall hear your music and see your thoughts.

Sanders' big house became more and more crowded. Animals came from the other side of the hill and even further away. They carried suitcases and duffel bags and cheerfully sat down at the long tables in the living-room. They had all heard that a big party was going on in the house, a party that would last for ever. They at once became members of the Josie Club.

'We have come to comfort Josie,' they said, 'because we have never seen the sea, nor the little harbour. We have heard lots of good things about them.'

They also wanted to know where they could hire boats.

Wherever Josie went, there were strange animals sitting, walking and lying down. They winked at her and cried:

'Comfort, Josie, comfort! Your soldier will be back soon, we know that for certain. Comfort!'

They did as the boss said. They did not cry too easily. They did not break the furniture, and outside, the kingfisher was still on the look-out.

Josie looked for a place where she could be alone. She rustled by strange feathers, stumbled over the smallest animals, which shot away from under her feet, was startled by the fieldmice in the sink, the moles under her blankets and the cobweb-fine humming birds that zoomed round the lamp. Even the desert fox had come. He sat at the window and let the light of the setting sun shine through his ears, so that he looked like a vase with two great pink flowers sticking out of it.

That evening the soldier played his harmonica.

Josie listened to the sad songs he played and saw what he was thinking. He was thinking of Josie: she was sitting in the big chair by the window, looking out over the sea.

Josie ran to the chair. There was a fat seal lying on it.

'Do you mind if I sit here?' asked Josie. 'He wants me to sit here.'

'Comfort!' said the seal, sliding off the chair.

Josie tipped the desert fox off the windowsill.

'He wants me to look out over the sea,' she said.

'Comfort!' said the desert fox.

Josie sat down and looked out over the sea. She listened to the sad songs the soldier was playing and saw suddenly that she was wearing the wrong dress!

She ran upstairs and opened her wardrobe. A snoring bear tumbled out and went on sleeping on the floor. Josie pulled on the right dress and ran back to the chair. Seven rats were tumbling on the thick cushion. Josie chased them away:

'He wants me to sit here.'

'Comfort!' giggled the rats, running off in seven directions.

Josie sat down, listened to the sad songs the soldier played and saw what he was thinking. He was thinking of Josie: she was sitting under the chestnut tree, her back against the trunk, smiling.

Josie began with the smile. Then she jumped up and ran outside. Six geese were doing a round dance under the tree.

'Come and dance with us!' they shrieked. 'We are one short . . . Join the circle. Dance with your head back and you'll forget everything. Dance with your head out and you'll only cry in the morning. And if you keep on dancing, then . . .'

Josie broke through the circle.

'He wants me to sit here!'

'Comfort!' cried the geese.

They closed the circle and danced on. Josie sat down, her back against the trunk. She closed her eyes and smiled; she listened to the sad songs the soldier played and saw what he was thinking. He was thinking of Josie: she was sitting under the chestnut tree with her back against the trunk and knitting little clothes. Her fingers wound the wool deftly round the needles, her hands resting on her big stomach.

Josie opened her eyes and looked at her stomach. She did not need to look. She could already feel it. Warm inside her womb, a baby tossed and turned. Oh, she thought, if only my soldier comes back before the baby is born. But she had seen his dreams when he sailed away on the black ship and knew that he would not come back. He wants me to smile, she thought, and she smiled.

She sheared wool from the sheep and made a spinning-wheel. The hedgehog was the spindle, three bats the wheel.

'He wants me to knit little clothes,' she said.

The animals approved of everything as long as they could go on comforting. The wheel hummed as it spun, the spindle wagged like a mad thing, and the soldier played the song 'I Saw My Lady Weep' – so sadly . . .

Josie shut her eyes and saw what he was thinking. He was thinking of Josie: she was a little girl again. She sat in the tree-house she had built long ago, high up in the chestnut tree. She was wearing a white dress again, sitting in the doorway, her legs tossing in the wild wind. She was reading the second part of the book that had everything in it. Leaves rustled past her, brown chestnut leaves as big as hands reaching for her, but she did not look up from the book . . . That was what the soldier thought as he longed for Josie.

Josie jumped up. She must go to the cellar, to the boxes full of little white dresses, to make one big dress out of the little ones, for her to wear, because that was what her soldier wanted. Her stomach was plump and round and she could feel the baby kicking, and kicking is good for a baby, so it has to have space.

But Josie could not get into the house. Animals, furred and feathered, were standing in the doorways, and even the windows were bulging. The animals had all come, from every country, from all the stars, all the animals, all of them, to the great comfort party.

Only Cousin Donkey was not there. Cousin Donkey had withdrawn to the stable. With the door locked, to be sure; he let no one in, not he. Only Josie, Josie would be allowed in if she wanted to come. But Josie didn't come, because her soldier never thought of her with Cousin Donkey in the stable.

The cellar window was ajar. The cellar was empty; the only thing there was a wall of boxes. The boxes were wobbling. Josie tried to set them straight, but they tumbled over her and everything was dark. Josie could hear her heart beating as if it was far away, in the boxes, or still further away, in the corners of the cellar: a heavy heartbeat, like the badger's bell ringing. She tried to escape from under the boxes. They were heavy and it was difficult, but she succeeded. She stood naked in the cellar. Quickly she pulled on a white dress. It fitted perfectly. She was a little girl again.

Behind the fallen boxes, in the place where the cannon had been, there was now a wardrobe, a wooden wardrobe, so beautiful . . .

'Sanders?' whispered Josie.

She looked about her, but there was no one there. Above her the animals were carrying on. They were stamping their feet.

'Comfort for Josie!' they shouted. 'Comfort for Josie! Comfort for Josie! . . .'

The floor above Josie's head billowed like new ice. It would not hold much longer. Josie ran to the wardrobe and tried to pull the door open.

She wanted to hide. But the door was locked. There was a keyhole, surrounded by elegant golden metalwork, but there was no key. The floor was billowing like a trampoline. Wood was cracking. Splinters shot through the cellar. Josie pressed her back against the wardrobe and shut her eyes. What was her soldier thinking now? What song was he playing?

Josie was too late. From the harmonica came only a single icy screech and the soldier had no more thoughts. Josie felt the note from the harmonica as pain in her body. She was growing, and the pain was everywhere. Then the sound disappeared over the horizon. Everything turned black and silent. Her soldier was dead.

Josie opened her eyes. The cellar was silent, and so were the rooms above it. The floor lay calmly on the beams. Josie was grown-up again, the baby tossing and turning in her stomach. She climbed the cellar steps.

The house was empty. The animals had vanished, all of them, back to the stars, the distant lands, the little harbour from which they came. Had they also heard the last note of the harmonica? Of course that wasn't possible.

No, they had fled from the Tar Men, with their chalk-white faces, who stood in the middle of the room. They said nothing, the Tar Men. Nor did they need to. Josie knew what they had to say and they knew that Josie knew. They gave her a black envelope. There was a letter in it – *Your soldier is dead* – and the key to the wardrobe in the cellar.

Seven

Josie thought she knew everything about death. Sanders had died, hadn't he? And oh! she still remembered it so well. But she was young then and Sanders was old . . . Now everything was different.

One by one the animals came back. Not the animals from the stars and the land behind the hill, they did not come, the party was over. No, the animals from the little harbour town. They came to comfort Josie. They trudged up the hill through the raw autumn and knocked at the door.

'Comfort, Josie,' they said softly.

But Josie did not want to hear anything more about comfort. Her grief was so great that every word hurt her.

'Soldiers do die,' she said. 'We might have known. You might have known. I might have known. Soldiers exist in order to die. What else are they good for? So they die. Logical, isn't it?'

She shut the door in their beaks or muzzles. Her heart was stiff. It beat only by dribs and drabs, and that hurt. She stood by the window of her bedroom and watched the sorrowful animals until they vanished into the little town. She fell on her bed. At once it seemed to be summer. The windows stood open and the curtains drifted in the breeze that came from the sea. She heard the tinkling sounds of the things hanging on the ropes down below on the quay, she heard the waves making their way into the little harbour, she felt the wind in her hair.

It's a dream, she thought, it's a dream! Now I am awake I must *stay* awake . . .

She wanted to escape from the dream, not because her soldier was dead, because he was not dead, she suddenly knew that for certain, her soldier was lying beside her, sleeping in his warm body. No, she was afraid she was going to hurt the animals again. And she did not want to. Never. Not even in a dream.

I must stay awake, thought Josie, I must stay awake, I must . . . But she fell asleep again. The dream dragged her along and she didn't know she was dreaming.

She was standing before the wardrobe in the cellar, holding in one hand the letter from the Tar Men, and in the other the golden key. She put the key in the lock and opened the door.

The wardrobe was full of secret drawers and doors and double bottoms; the wardrobe was rather like a house, with attics and cellars and servants' rooms, alcoves and stairways, kitchens and wardrobes. There were so many secret rooms, a spider that went in would never find its way out again.

Josie put the letter from the Tar Men in a drawer. She closed the drawer and locked the door of the wardrobe. And at the moment when she turned the key it was as if a flame shot through her heart. Her blood began to flow again! Josie lifted her head and sang. She sang Cousin Donkey's silly wedding song. All her grief had fallen away. She had not forgotten her soldier, only her grief at his death.

Cautiously she reopened the wardrobe and took the letter out of the drawer. She became heavy inside and tears pressed against her eyelids. So that's how it works, she thought. She quickly replaced the letter. Drawer shut. Door closed. Wardrobe locked. Gone is gone. Her grief stayed behind in the wardrobe. Not for ever, thought Josie. Later it can come out again, later, when I can manage the grief. And she sang again.

'Why are you singing?' asked a voice by the cellar window. Josie saw the kingfisher's face.

'Have you been standing there listening to me?' she asked angrily.

'I'm on the look-out,' said the kingfisher. 'It's very important – that's why I do it. But the world has grown so cold . . . that's why I look out from inside now.'

'Oh,' said Josie.

'Don't you want to cry?' asked the kingfisher.

'My grief is in the wardrobe,' Josie explained. 'Not for ever. For the time being . . .'

'Handy,' said the kingfisher.

'But don't tell the others,' said Josie. 'Or they'll all be standing on the doorstep with their grief tomorrow.'

But they were already there. Because they all had sorrows and they wanted to be rid of them.

'Come in,' said Josie.

'Wipe your feet!' cried the kingfisher. 'Would you believe, Josie, that yesterday I almost bit my wing . . .? I was *so* sorrowful!'

The animals came inside, carrying their grief. Josie saw that grief that looks small can be very big, and grief that looks big can be quite small. She stuffed all the animals' grief in her wardrobe and locked the door

firmly. Only the kingfisher's grief she hung on the coatstand.

The animals ran to and fro with their grief. You had to get there before it had gone, otherwise it was no good. They had to hurry.

'Come and collect it again when you can manage it,' said Josie.

But none of the animals would take back their grief. On the contrary, they brought more and more. They brought small griefs: falls, scraped knee, cut thumb, a fishing-rod broken when the pike pulled on it, balloon flown away, envious or lost, dinosaur extinct, broken doll, fallen over in the bath, marbles vanished, fear of the poor old bat that never harmed anyone, grief over a brother who cried so much, for instance because he had fallen, scraped his knee, cut his thumb and broken a fishing-rod when the pike pulled on it . . . Small griefs came neatly smoothed in tidy piles on the floorboards.

They brought great grief: the death of friends and mothers and fathers, fear of storms and ghosts and old tales; the animals came with regret for their misdeeds and grief for the punishment they had received, they came with war and fire and a child abandoned, and sometimes they had been far from home, alone, and much too long. The great grief took its place like heavy winter coats in the hanging section of the wardrobe.

They also brought secret grief. They came in, shifty and ashamed, they had hidden their grief in boxes and towels and newspapers. They handed it over quickly and ran out of the door. Josie hid the grief between the double bottoms of the drawers, where other people keep silver knives and forks and spoons. Against thieves.

It was very dull. They had nothing more to talk about, Josie and the animals. The animals greeted her: 'Lovely autumn,' and Josie replied: 'Wonderful, yes.' She hid their grief away in her wardrobe and they ran out of the door again, their hats pulled down firmly on their heads, into the raw autumn storm.

Eight

Then winter came. It was snowing. Josie stood at the window and hummed strange songs. She made them up herself. The tunes hummed into her mouth, the words were left behind in her head. Anyone who heard her wouldn't be able to make out what she was singing. But no one heard her. She was alone. The snowstorm kept the animals inside. That caused them great distress, but the distress could wait until the storm died down.

Josie stood at the window, looking at the gravestone under the chestnut tree. Sanders lay buried there . . .

Sanders, the old carpenter, who had taken her into his house, this house; the dear pig who had taught her so much, with whom she had been so happy, so safe.

Until one day, in the winter, snow was lying . . . that sorrowful story.

She sang more beautifully as she thought of it. She hummed, and just as she was about to sing the words as well, she knew for certain that Sanders was standing behind her.

'I was just thinking of you,' she said.

'That's what I thought,' said Sanders.

Josie turned. There was no one there. And yet the voice had sounded so clear! No one. But on the floor stood Sanders' big, richly decorated toolbox containing the shining, razor-sharp chisels and saws and the dully gleaming hammers and nails. The child kicked happily inside her and Josie knew that it was time to make a cradle.

She sawed and carpentered and chiselled, just as Sanders used to do. The wood shavings flew about and the most wonderful smell Josie knew spread through the room: the smell of fresh wood. She heard Sanders laughing. Not behind her, not in front of her, not above her or below her, but somewhere deep in her memory. The cradle would be the most elegant ever made in this world.

Josie sang from a full heart. A wonderful song:

> *'On the sloping meadows high*
> *There the moping Sleddows lie.'*

But Josie had no idea what Sleddows could be. Were they animals, dream animals? Or people, the Sleddow family, whom she did not know? Who would lie moping on sloping meadows? She ran to find Cousin Donkey. He knew about beautiful words in lines, with music attached.

Cousin Donkey was in the stable, sitting on a stool and staring ahead of him. Josie sang her song to him.

'What are Sleddows?' asked Cousin Donkey.

'I don't know,' said Josie crossly.

Cousin Donkey was sitting there so glumly!

'Don't sit there so glumly!' she said.

Cousin Donkey shrugged his shoulders.

'I shall sing it again,' said Josie.

'I'd rather you didn't,' said Cousin Donkey. 'I don't like hearing you sing.'

'Well!' said Josie.

She was getting crosser and crosser.

'I'm grieving,' said Cousin Donkey.

'Give it up,' said Josie, 'and I'll stuff it in the wardrobe.'

Cousin Donkey shook his head. 'My grief,' he said, 'doesn't belong in your wardrobe. It wouldn't even fit in your wardrobe!'

'All grief fits in the wardrobe,' said Josie.

'One grief doesn't.'

'What grief is that?'

'My grief,' said Cousin Donkey.

'Oh,' said Josie.

'Because I am grieved,' said Cousin Donkey, '*about* the wardrobe . . .'

'I don't understand,' said Josie.

'I know that,' said Cousin Donkey. 'When you're not grieving you don't understand anything. That's well known . . . So I'm going away.'

That frightened Josie.

'I don't want you to!' she cried.

'Just stuff your grief in the wardrobe,' said Cousin Donkey.

He stood up.

'But why?' asked Josie.

'You're not crying any more,' said Cousin Donkey. 'I liked you so much when you were crying.'

'Well, I see!' shouted Josie furiously. 'So I have to go and cry a bit because you enjoy it?'

'Certainly,' said Cousin Donkey.

'Then get lost!' shouted Josie. 'You just go and find someone else who wants to cry for you.'

Cousin Donkey walked down the hill and Josie watched him going.

'I'm doing good to the animals!' she cried.

Cousin Donkey did not look round.

Josie ran to the cellar and pulled open the big door of the wardrobe. The drawers, the shelves and even the hanging section, all of them were bursting with grief. She began to clear a space for her own grief about Cousin Donkey's departure. Cousin Donkey, her oldest friend . . . and suddenly she began to hunt through the whole wardrobe like a madwoman, from top to bottom, deep into the secret places, but wherever she looked, she could not find Cousin Donkey's grief anywhere . . . And she had only just realised!

'Josie . . .?' said a voice behind her.

Josie closed the door of the wardrobe and looked round. There was the young buffalo.

'The Josie Club,' he said. 'All the animals . . . would so much like just once . . . at least if you wouldn't mind . . . as long as you wouldn't get cross . . . because we asked, I mean . . . in other words, if you don't get cross and you don't mind, then . . .'

'Lovely weather,' said Josie.

'Yes, beautiful,' said the young buffalo.

He looked awkwardly at his hooves.

'Call them,' said Josie.

'They're here already,' said the buffalo.

And it was true. Above their heads, in the room upstairs, there was whispering and shuffling and scrabbling. A chair fell over.

'We have lit a fire,' said the buffalo.

Nine

The fire in the hearth was blazing up. The flames seemed to be waving flags of red and blue and yellow, and hats of smoke. As if it was a party! But the animals in the room were looking pensive. No one was laughing. It was a long time since there had been laughter in the big house on the hill, and in the little town by the harbour, too.

The badger jumped off the chair by the window. Josie must sit there. It was a good idea, with her big tummy. The kangaroo poked the fire. He did it very skilfully. The old bat hung from the lamp. The other animals sat round the hearth. They were all looking at Josie.

The young buffalo began to speak.

'Josie,' he said, 'we have come to collect our grief.'

'I haven't!' shrieked the kingfisher.

'Yes,' said the buffalo, 'you too.'

'It almost makes me cry,' said the kingfisher.

The buffalo scratched his mighty throat.

'We want to thank you, Josie,' he said, 'for what you have done for us. But you know, we so much want to be happy again. And without grief we can't . . .'

'Well, I can!' wept the kingfisher.

'Go and stand look-out,' said the sheep.

'What about,' said the kingfisher, 'opening the wardrobe one day, and then closing it the next? Closed for me and Josie, open for you . . .'

'Josie,' said the buffalo. 'We want to ask you to open the wardrobe. We would like to have our grief back again.'

The animals nodded silently.

'We were so alone. No one came to comfort us, because we had no grief. We would rather have some grief, and then comfort, and then have fun together. And with you, Josie; we miss you so.'

And Josie nodded. She looked at the buffalo. He was still young, yet he looked like Sanders. He was so quiet, and so kind. She thought about her grief over the death of Sanders and she *cared* so much for that grief. But she did not know how to say it.

74

'Grief must come back into the world, Josie,' said the buffalo. 'Once you've forgotten your grief, what you still remember is not worth much either. We want to comfort you again.'

'Do I have to cry?' asked Josie. 'You're just like Cousin Donkey!'

The buffalo looked at his hooves.

'We could make another wardrobe!' cried the kingfisher. 'And that wardrobe can always be open – to all the animals. And the wardrobe in the cellar can stay shut for ever – for me and for Josie.'

'Did Cousin Donkey send you?' asked Josie.

'No,' said the buffalo, 'we wanted this ourselves. For a long time. But it was so kind of you to have our grief in your wardrobe as well . . . we didn't dare to say so.'

'So why now, then?' asked Josie.

'Cousin Donkey said it was possible now . . .'

Silence fell in the room. No one dared to draw breath. The silence lasted as long as you could hold your breath.

Josie thought of Sanders again. Josie often thought of Sanders and then she grieved. But she had never put that grief in the wardrobe. Never! No question of it! It had come so long ago, and she was used to it. It had become part of her memories. And also of herself. It would not be good to think about Sanders without the grief as well. It would not be *honest*. Sanders had been so kind . . . It seemed that everything Josie had experienced with him was more beautiful *with* grief, and that through her grief she cared for him more when she thought of him. Her memories of Sanders would be the poorer without grief.

'Right,' said Josie, 'the wardrobe shall be opened.'

A storm seemed to break out in the room. All the pent-up breath puffed out of the beaks and the muzzles. The flames in the hearth suddenly flattened out backwards, like hair with grease on it.

'Ahem,' said the buffalo.

The storm died down. The buffalo winked, and from a corner the badger took a large piece of cloth stretched on a framework of laths. He turned it over. It was a painting – a portrait of the soldier. A perfect likeness. It was wonderful.

'This is a present,' said the buffalo. 'From all of us. I'm not allowed to say who did it, because the painter is dreadfully shy.'

Well, that was true. The snowy owl's face turned so red that it was awful to behold.

Josie looked at the painting. Just for a moment. She could not look longer. She wanted to say something, but her throat closed up. It was as if the wardrobe were already open. She looked out of the window. The snow had gone, the chestnut tree bore pink flowers, the child turned over inside her. It was time.

She walked down the cellar steps. She opened the wardrobe wide. She took out her grief and wept. She wept for her soldier.

The animals comforted her.

After that the animals themselves went into the cellar and came up again one by one. The wardrobe really was open. The animals flung themselves sobbing on the floor.

Josie was the first to cry herself out. She sat up straight in her chair, looked about her and said:

'There. And now I want to kiss.'

The animals went on crying. They looked lovingly at Josie, but their tears kept flowing. Anyone crying so hard and kissing at the same time is quite likely to drown. Only the kingfisher was not crying. He stood in one corner of the room and thought.

'Right,' he said, after a pause. 'What must be, must be. I don't mind kissing . . . but not all over each other. I'll kiss here, you kiss there. No getting too close!'

And then the buffalo began to laugh. From his throat came a huge bellow of enjoyment. The sheep was laughing too. And the kangaroo. And the duck. The old bat could not hang on to the lamp for laughing. He fluttered down and landed on the badger's head.

The badger roared with laughter. HA HA HA HA HA HA HA, heavy and bronze like the booming of his bell.

So the room filled with laughter and cackling, snorting and cheering. The animals looked at each other: they were all still lying on the floor, only the old bat hung over the badger's head like a mop. Tears of grief turned into tears of pleasure. Never had there been such laughter in the big house on the hill.

The kingfisher stole out of the room. He took his umbrella from the coatstand in the passage. He did not see that his grief was hanging there too. He couldn't see it. He could almost see it. He walked down the hill to the little harbour, muttering to himself, which was why he did not hear the sudden silence that fell in Sanders' house.

For there, in the room, three black shadows had fallen over the animals hugging each other on the floor.

'The Tar Men!'

The war was over and won. The king had stolen and plundered and robbed, and now the Tar Men had come to distribute money. Anyone who had a dead soldier got a hundred coins.

'We buy your grief with it,' they said. 'Then you're rid of it. Your grief is still in the wardrobe, isn't it?'

'Grief is not for sale,' said a voice.

'Cousin Donkey!' cried Josie.

And so it was. He stood in the doorway, looking amazingly angry.

'Out!' he shouted.

The Tar Men rattled a sackful of coins.

'Out!!!' shouted Cousin Donkey.

It looked as if the Tar Men were laughing. The mouths in their chalk-white faces were slightly ajar, and a sound like tearing paper came out.

'The wardrobe is empty,' said Josie. 'If you wait a moment I'll give you back the key.'

But the Tar Men did not have a chance to wait.

The young buffalo sprang up, fuming, turned about and gave the men such an enormous kick on their backsides with his hind legs that they flew out of the window, over the little town, and landed on their ship

with such a mighty thud that the anchor chain broke
and the black ship sailed out of the harbour as if towed
by a thousand furious dolphins.

Josie looked out of the window and saw the ship
vanishing into the distance, still at such speed that it
seemed to be toppling over the horizon. Josie turned
round.

'Cousin Donkey,' she said.

And then she got her kiss after all.

The baby's little fists hammered jealously against
her inside. There would not be long to wait for the first
kiss, Josie could feel that clearly.

The animals said goodbye and skipped, singing and whistling, down the hill. Only the sheep stayed with Josie. She thought that was wise. She put big pans of water on the stove and began to fold little clothes. As soon as she had a pile of them she tied a jolly blue ribbon round them.

Josie hung up the painting of the soldier in her bedroom. She looked at it and cried. She was glad she had known him, that he had loved her, and she him, that he had been her soldier. She crept into bed.

Cousin Donkey laid damp cloths on her forehead and her wrists and the sheep looked after the rest. Then Josie's baby was born. It was a little boy. Josie gave him the kiss he had been longing for, and a hundred more. With the baby safe in her arms she fell asleep.

Ten

Josie woke up in the arms of her soldier. She kissed him gently on his sleeping eyes and released herself from his embrace.

'Swan,' he murmured.

What a long time since I heard that name, thought Josie.

She ran to the window. The morning promised a sparkling day. Above the little harbour hung a thin mist. It looked like a painting. It looked . . . as if the painter's baby had upset his mug of milk over the painting and the milk had mingled with the paint, which was still wet – that light. The dew on the fields steamed and the sunlight shone through. It was, Josie thought, as if she were looking through tears. So beautiful.

The world was still silent. She heard the smallest and most distant sounds. The wavelets rippled into the harbour and on the quay someone was growling bad words. A coach was tipped up and set back on its wheels again. Moaning and groaning and creaking. It must be Cousin Donkey! Cousin Donkey, who could write such beautiful poems, was now busy saying the most awful things, as if he had turned the dictionary on its head. His dragging footsteps moved along the little streets of the town, up the hill, the creaking wheels of the coach following him.

'Slept well, Cousin?' cawed the voice of the kingfisher.

'I'm not your cousin,' growled Cousin Donkey. 'You sitting, peeking again?'

'I'm standing watch,' said the kingfisher. 'It has to be done.'

'I wish you would stand on your glasses,' said Cousin Donkey.

'It's important for someone to stay on the look-out,' said the kingfisher. 'It's very important. That's why I'm doing it.'

Josie started. She had dreamed that too! She smiled. It was a beautiful dream. That her soldier was dead then was sad; she was glad he was alive but . . . Suddenly she felt a tremendous longing for her baby.

She wanted to see him again. She wanted to rock him in her arms again before the day began. Perhaps she would succeed if she went on dreaming . . .

She crept in again beside her soldier and leafed through the second part of the book which had everything in it. She wasn't really reading, she was still sleepy. Without falling asleep again, she saw the whole of her dream once more, in memory: she saw the Tar Men coming up the hill again, holding in their hands the letter for her soldier, and so it began and she saw everything in detail, until the moment when she rocked her baby in her arms and kissed and kissed and kissed.

And when, after nearly a year, she had a son, whom she named Alexander, she told him her dream. He laughed about it when he was nought, he laughed about it when he was one, and when he was two, and when he was three he toddled out of the house, and down the hill, to the little harbour.

He sat down on a barrel on the quay and told the animals about the dream. He knew the whole story by heart and the animals thought it was wonderful.

'Come and listen!' they cried to everyone who was not already listening. 'We are all in Josie's dream.'

'Jossie?' asked the boy.

'Josie,' said the buffalo.

The boy nodded.

'Jossie,' he said.

The kingfisher shook his head. 'It can't turn out well,' he said, 'such a little child so close to the water.'

But the buffalo thought it could.

'As long as we take good care,' he said.

And they did.

The boy had to tell the story seven times over. After that the buffalo picked him up and carried him up to the big wooden house on the hill. Josie stood in the doorway.

'Jossie,' said the child.

'Josie,' said the buffalo.

'Swan,' said Josie. 'That is what Papa calls me, isn't it?'

'To us,' said the buffalo, 'you are Josie, and Josie you will remain . . .'

Josie smiled.

And her son called her Jossie.

Book Three

JOSIE'S
SONG

Eleven

'You must learn to skate,' Sanders had told Josie long ago, 'otherwise you will start complaining about the ice when you're old.'

The old carpenter had made skates for her, of steel and gleaming wood, with tips that always pointed towards Josie, however she twirled and slipped, however she fell, and Josie skated with Sanders and Cousin Donkey and after that with her soldier. All three were now dead. But Josie had not complained when the ice came – big ice floes that floated into the little harbour like giant hockey pucks and crept up against the quay.

Just as the ice came, so it went away again. As it always does. A duster of light passed over everything, the buds on the trees sprang open at the speed of light, and the flowers spread their petals to catch all that light. The light even found its way into the sounds that rose clearly from the little harbour to the window at which Josie was sitting. For the first time that year it stood wide open.

The ancient kingfisher was on the look-out. On the quay. He looked over the sea, along the coastline to the south, to the hill on which Josie's house stood, to the coastline to the north and then across the sea again. His eyes crossed the world like the light from a lighthouse and the vertebrae in his neck creaked. A hedgehog came tottering in from the south, on legs still stiff from his winter sleep.

'Good spring,' he said. 'More beautiful dreams this winter?'

'I don't dream any more,' said the kingfisher. 'I'm often deceived.'

He was so old that no one knew for certain if he had ever been born, so old that no one knew for certain if he would ever die. Grumble-guts don't go in for dying.

'I dreamed that it was always April the first,' announced the hedgehog. 'Boy, how I laughed!'

'And?' asked the kingfisher.

'And what?' asked the hedgehog.

'And . . . is it the first of April today?'

'No idea,' said the hedgehog, 'just got up.'

'No!' cried the kingfisher. 'It's April the second and tomorrow it's April the third and the day after tomorrow, April the fourth . . . It's almost always *not* the first of April!'

'Until the day after spring,' muttered the hedgehog.

He tottered off, along the quay to the north, with tiny dry leaves of laughter stuck on his prickles. Josie heard his feet passing like kisses over the cobbles.

'All deceit!' the kingfisher shouted after him. 'I know, because I dreamed all the dreams, all of them; I was the first to dream them, because I was on the

look-out. The last dream was the worst; I dreamed of a ship full of new dreams . . .'

The hedgehog turned into an alley.

Josie sat by the open window, laying out cards on a table, side by side, very neatly. A row of seven over a row of eight, a row of six over the row of seven, five over six, four over five, three over four, two over three, one over two . . . The rest of the cards she placed in a pile. Very neatly.

The kingfisher raised his wing to his eyes and stared towards the horizon. '. . . and after that,' he muttered, 'I never dreamed anything again.'

Josie smiled. She turned a card. Ace of spades. She had played this game before, when her soldier was away at war and she was waiting for him. She always won then. She knew tricks that were not allowed. But since her soldier had died she had not won again. She played with her hands alone, her head no longer joined in.

'I'm going to make something beautiful for you,' the soldier had told her.

'I love you,' said Josie.

'In the cellar,' said the soldier. 'It's a secret. You can't look until I tell you.'

'And when's that?'

'When it's ready.'

'And when will it be ready?'

'When it works.'

'And when will it work?'

'When I say you can look.'

The soldier had come back from his last war and lowered his cannon into the cellar. There he started work. He worked day and night, until he was older than he had ever been. Josie sat by the open window and read from the third part of the book which had everything in it. She had inherited it from Cousin Donkey. Sometimes such a hellish row rose up from the cellar that Josie closed the book and went down to the harbour to talk to the buffalo.

Since her soldier was dead she hadn't read any more. She still had one chapter to go.

'I've hidden the key to the cellar.'

'Well, I'm not going to look for it,' said Josie.

'I know that,' said the soldier. 'That's why I've hidden it very badly.'

Sixty-four days ago he was dead and he had never told Josie that she could go into the cellar. Fifty-six days ago they had buried him.

The path to the graveyard on the hill was stiff with ice. With scouring pads under their feet Josie and the animals clambered up. Herons carried the coffin. They stuck their toes deep into the ice and never wobbled.

Josie followed, on the buffalo's arm. She would have preferred to walk behind the procession to pick up anyone who slid away, but that would not do, he was her soldier and she belonged in front. No one had spoken at the graveside. The animals dared not, they thought Josie could do it better, and Josie did want to say something, yes, she wanted to say everything, but only to her soldier, and she couldn't do that, because her soldier was dead.

Since the burial Josie had not left her house. She sat on the chair at the table by the window. She had not searched for the key. She dealt cards again and again.

Two of hearts.

Josie had often longed to be old. You didn't have to do anything, because no one told you what to do; you could do anything, because no one told you there was anything you couldn't do; you could do everything you liked . . . but there was no one left to do everything with. You could think of the past, but to whom could you tell all the things you remembered? You were too stiff to climb up to your tree-house . . .

The scent of warm grass wafted in through the window, the buds of the chestnut tree burst pinkly open and the hawthorn tree swayed whitely in the

light. And Josie saw it all and Josie smelled it all, but the light got no further than her eyes, the scent no further than her nose.

She dealt the three of hearts.

Her son had gone, long since, over the sea with his sweetheart. They lived there now, with their children and grandchildren. Josie saw them growing and swarming through the letters she received. Once a year their ship came into the little harbour, and sometimes twice – if someone they cared about had died. Josie had never found it hard that they lived so far away: 'The umbilical cord is cut,' she said, 'the heart's cord never.'

But now . . .

For the first time that year the sun climbed so high in the sky that its rays falling through the leaded panes above the open window no longer made flashes of yellow and red and blue dance on the ceiling, nor on the far, white wall, but on a corner of the table. On the book that lay there. Josie picked it up. Coloured swirls of dust rose up. Between the leaves a bright piece of card stuck out. She pulled it out of the book; after all, she knew how far she had got.

In her hand she held the king of hearts.

So that was why the game never came out! Josie was angry. She didn't know she could still do that. She was angry with the game, with the card, with her soldier because he was dead and, above all, angry with herself. Because she sat waiting.

Josie had never waited before. She did not wait for the swan to carry her to the quay, she paddled; she did not wait for the soldier to fall in love with her, she made him fall in love, with her and no one else; even in her dreams she had never waited. And now she sat waiting, and the longer she waited, the longer grew the days, and the longer the days grew, the longer the waiting lasted. And what was she waiting for . . .? Was she waiting for her soldier to tell her she could look in the cellar?

She stood up and searched, but did not find the key.

She fell asleep, sitting upright in the chair that Sanders had made. For the first time since the death of her soldier she slept deeply, not disturbed by memories that tipped her, like high waves, out of her sleep and made her start awake with the feeling that all that was good lay behind her and would never return. She slept. Twilight crept through the room in big grey socks, and there was talking down on the quay.

'We are expected,' said three voices.

'It only looks like that,' said the kingfisher. 'I'm standing here, but I'm not expecting anything. I haven't been expecting anything for ages. I'm on the look-out. I saw you coming from a distance. Your ship looked small, now I can see that it's big.'

'We haven't come for you,' said the men. 'We've come for the old woman.'

'But Josie belongs to us!'

The men grinned. Their faces were white as chalk, their lips whiter still, almost blue – as if carved from moonlight.

'I . . . I . . . I don't know her,' mumbled the kingfisher. 'I don't know where she lives.'

'We know her. She called us once in a dream for someone else, and later in a dream of her own. The third time there is no need to call. Waiting is enough.'

The light of the setting sun sailed red upon the water. The men dragged sticks through the redness and the sticks turned into flaming torches. The kingfisher turned towards the hill. He saw the house, the open window and Josie. He did not see that she was asleep.

'Josie!' he shouted. 'Josie! Josie!!!'

The men walked up the hill, following the kingfisher's cries.

Josie started awake and saw them coming, three beings dressed in black under a banner of fire. She saw what she had been waiting for: 'The Tar Men.'

A chill breeze blew the cards off the table. Josie stood up and walked down the passage to the cellar door.

The key was in the lock.

Twelve

Josie shut the door, locked it, crick-crack, and sat down on the top step. It was dark in the cellar. Rosy light came in through only one, far-off little window. Josie thought about her soldier. In her memory she saw him standing there, beside his bronze cannon, his mouth was moving, but he made no sound. Josie read the words on his lips: 'For you, only for you.'

Bronze balls rolled over the ground, to the furthest corners of the cellar and back again, following each other in circles; there were balls as small as a pinhead, and balls as big as a sleeping hedgehog.

So this is it, thought Josie. My soldier made this for me, only for me.

The balls rose up and wafted through the room, as

stately as ladies and gentlemen seeking their places for the dance; some radiated light, others absorbed it and threw it back again – as happens with dancers when love is involved.

Josie sat on the steps on the edge of the universe and looked at everything that existed and would exist for ever: the stars and planets and their moons and the misty Milky Way, in a cellar on a planet amidst stars and planets and their moons and the misty Milky Way, in – Josie knew that suddenly for certain – a cellar on a planet amidst stars and planets and their moons and the misty Milky Way . . .

She was startled by tapping. A branch of the chestnut tree bowed low and knocked at the little window, like a salesman with a basket of flowers.

So her soldier had succeeded. He had made something for her, it was ready, and it worked. But then, why had he never asked her to come and look?

Josie drew a deep breath and a flame of grief blazed up in her heart. He had never asked her because he thought that it was *not* finished, because it did not work when *he* looked at it . . . because he did not know that it would be really finished only when Josie looked at it.

You can make things that are as beautiful and splendid as you like, but they do not really exist until someone else looks at them and also finds them beautiful and splendid. You can caress, but if there is no one there to caress, your hand stays in the air. You can comfort, but if there is no one there to comfort, your words blow away on the clouds, which have no need of comfort. You can live, but if no one lives with you, you are not alive. And if, when your end comes, no one is sitting, wild with grief, by your bed – are you really dead? Who can say . . . And, thought Josie, if someone *is* sitting by your deathbed, someone who cared and cares very much for you and will remember you, then you're not dead, either.

'It is ready,' whispered Josie. 'It works.'

The words tickled the corners of her mouth. She smiled and went down the steps like a toddler, on her bottom, step by step, and set her feet on the mud floor. She stood up and walked into the universe. She plucked the earth from its voyage round the sun, carefully, as if the little bronze ball were a bird. The ball turned white and it was winter.

From the inn by the harbour came music, the tinkling of glasses and clamour of voices. It was evening, the hill was already hidden in darkness, but the lanterns on the quay were alight.

Snowflakes whirled in the lamplight and children

whirled on the cobbles of the quay. Ice floes lay like slides against the quayside.

Josie lay flat on her sleigh, above an ice floe. Cousin Donkey stood behind her.

'Off you go,' he said. 'However far you go, I'll hold on to you. Always.'

'I don't dare, unless you push me,' said Josie.

Cousin Donkey gave her a push and she shot down the floe on to the flat ice, towards the two piers which lay like a ballerina's arms round the harbour. The night blew through her hair. Just before the open water of the sea the sleigh stopped. The rope tied to the back of it was no longer than the harbour. The other end lay in the strong hands of Cousin Donkey. He began to wind it in, as fast as a tiny machine, and Josie glided backwards across the ice to the quay. The music and the hubbub in the inn came closer, she shot into the light. Cousin Donkey wound her up over the floes. She wanted to do it again, and then again, and Cousin Donkey let her.

'Off you go again,' he said. 'Have a good trip.'

'Wait a minute,' said Josie.

From the inn came a song. It was Sanders, his voice rising above all the rest. He sang an old song about oats growing in the fields.

Winter, thought Josie, is the loveliest season.

A snowflake fell on the little bronze ball in her hand and for a minute the cellar seemed full of glittering crystal, as if Josie were inside the snowflake. Then the snow melted. The ball turned pink and it was spring.

Josie sat under the flowering chestnut. She was still a little girl. Sanders stood beside her, carving a heart in the trunk of the tree. He carved an arrow, too, that passed through the heart, an arrow with a tip and a feather. Beside the feather he carved a J in the wood.

'But I'm not in love!' cried Josie.

'And don't you care for anyone?'

'Oh yes . . . Cousin Donkey and so on.'

'That's all right, then,' said Sanders.

'And also a tee-ee-ee-ee-eeny bit for you.'

'When you're as old as I am even a teeny little bit is very fine,' said Sanders.

'And a tee-ee-ee-ee-eeny little bit?'

'When you are as old as I am,' Sanders told her, 'one rose is enough for you. When you sniff the scent of the rose, you are smelling all the roses you have smelled in your whole life. In one drop of dew on a blade of grass you see all the rivers and seas you have ever travelled. In one tick of one clock you hear all the time you have lived through. Just give me one kiss . . . one is enough.'

Josie jumped up and kissed Sanders. The old carpenter smiled.

'And in one smile,' he said, 'you feel the pleasure of the whole world. Even if the smile is your own.'

He smiled so sweetly . . .

'Put in an S or something,' said Josie.

And Sanders carved an S by the tip of the arrow through the heart, in the trunk of the chestnut tree.

Spring, thought Josie, is the loveliest season.

One pink petal wafted down on to the little bronze ball in her hand. It sprang open like a bud, and grew, and the blossom filled the cellar to its furthest corners. Then the petal fell on the mud floor. The ball turned yellow and it was summer.

Josie stood by an open window, looking out over hilly slopes with trees as smooth as feathers which seemed not to have grown but to have been stuck in the ground. Above them blazed the sun. She was travelling with her soldier, the first long journey they had made together, and everything was new. The people, the animals, the way they moved as they spoke, and their language – like a tinkling musical box which, once you had wound it up, would never stop. Her soldier had made an early start into the hills. Josie had slept late.

In the distance a little figure was approaching. Josie leaned across the windowsill and shaded her eyes with her hand. It was he. In his hand he held a rose. Josie turned back to the little bedroom in the inn, straightened the bedspread, pushed the table to the window, set the chairs by it, took a scarf from her case, laid it on the table, filled the wine bottle which they had emptied the night before under the stars with water and set it by the window.

'You're just like a cat,' said the soldier.

Josie put the rose in the bottle and closed the shutters.

'You,' said the soldier, 'know how to make a cosy home out of the shabbiest corner.'

Josie began to purr. The soldier picked her up and carried her to the bed. Sunlight shone in through a chink. On the square in front of the inn children were playing. They laughed and called to each other, not in the language of the country but in the language of all children.

Summer, thought Josie, is the loveliest season.

The little voices carolled through the cellar. She fell asleep, the ball in her hand turned brown, and when she woke up it was autumn.

The storm came roaring in over the hill, bringing grey sacks full of leaves that it emptied out over the little town and round the house that Sanders had built. Josie had always found autumn the loveliest season. She liked the chestnuts and the acorns and the dolls you could make out of them. She liked the toadstools with their lopsided hats; she liked the first evening when the fire is lit and rain beats against the windows and the tiles rattle on the roof . . .

But now fear blew in with it over the hill.

Josie stood by the window. Over the harbour she saw herons flying, in rumpled coats. Her son lay in her arms. He was still so small, so young, his little bones were still so supple. He was as old as the flowers that were dying outside and being buried under brown leaves. Josie had always thought that to die was a misfortune, something that could happen, some time perhaps . . . to others. Now for the first time she saw that everything must die. Everyone. She too. Just now, when for the first time she must be immortal to look after her son.

The child thought everything was wonderful. He could not speak yet, but he pursed his lips and blew like the storm and with his tongue and his first teeth he imitated the leaves that tapped against the window. A dear little storm from his mouth blew away Josie's tears. Josie was so afraid of her fear that she began to comfort her son.

'Do you see how wonderfully it's all been planned, and how exactly the plan is carried out? The storm has picked up the fruit and seeds of plants and trees and blown them deep into the ground. It's as if in the autumn the world makes love to the earth. And when they're tired they sleep all winter under a coverlet of brown or white. They sleep and know that everything will live for ever; that the sadness of today covers up the cheerfulness until it blooms again in the spring, that death protects life.'

Josie sighed. It was as if she had been reading aloud from a book she didn't know. Everything she had said was new to her, and yet she had known at once that it was true.

Autumn, she thought, is the loveliest season after all.

Her son pursed his lips, a fierce gust of wind came from his mouth and blew a leaf into the air, so old the green had turned brown, the brown faded, only the veins flew through the air like a cobweb. The leaf came down on the ball in Josie's hand and grew as big as the cellar and Josie climbed on to the leaf and sailed away on the storm. She stared downwards, through the veins, she had never before seen the world from above, or had she . . .? A sense of long ago rose up in her, a safe feeling; it seemed as if she were coming home from a life-long journey. But the feeling did not turn into a memory.

She was surprised that time was so small. Everything she had known fitted into the palm of her hand. And yet it was more than enough. She closed her hand on the ball. The cellar grew dark. The window in the distance shone deep purple in the wall, but let in no more light. Cautiously Josie opened her hands. The ball was blue.

Josie sat on the bottom step in the cellar with a little blue ball in the bowl of her hands. She pulled a funny face and saw herself pulling a funny face, quick as if in a looking-glass. That was now. She saw herself standing up. That was in a little while. She herself was still sitting down.

She saw herself passing into the universe, leaving the world behind her, in her path around the sun. She ran to the cellar window. Pink and purple had given way to a sky of blue, the deepest blue that Josie had ever seen, nearly black, and in the blue the stars and planets and their moons and the misty Milky Way winked at her . . .

Josie had not known that blue could be such a warm colour.

She tried to open the window, but the metal of the frame had rusted in all the years when Sanders had not been there to oil it. Josie looked about her, saw an empty picture frame and used it to smash the glass into splinters.

The chestnut bough leaned inside, picked Josie up and set her down outside. There she stood, under all that blue. She filled her lungs with fresh air. Her whole body, from the smallest grey hair on her crown to the big bunion under her feet, was tingling. She was so happy, she did not know whom to thank. It made her so light, so light . . .

The earth could no longer hold her.

Thirteen

We sat at our table in the inn by the little harbour and looked out across the sea. We were drinking wine. Many members of the Josie Club had died, but we were still there.

'Shall I carry on?' asked the buffalo.

We nodded.

The buffalo read out the letter that Josie had sent us. The letter was old, but not as old as we were. It was kept inside the book which had everything in it. It was a thick book, so the letter stayed smooth, as good as new, however often it was read out:

> *Darlings all,*
> *They that bloom gaily in the spring*

And in the summer bear their fruit
In autumn have the warmest feet
And laugh into the winter.
A kiss from Josie.

'Beautiful,' sighed the snowy owl. He blushed under the feathers on his back.

'She is dead,' said the kingfisher. 'We must comfort her. Rule five.'

'She is not dead,' said the snowy owl. He wanted to take a sip but was shaking so hard that the glass broke when he put it to his bill.

'You're not allowed to break any furniture,' croaked the kingfisher. 'Rule three.'

'She is not dead,' said the hedgehog. 'She has gone away . . .'

This was an old conversation.

'She is dead,' said the kingfisher. 'Look here, I'm crying.'

It was a good thing he had said so, because no one could see it. His tears were made of dust.

'Don't cry too easily!' said the hedgehog sneakily. 'Rule two.'

'Josie was never born,' said the buffalo, 'which means she can't die, either.'

'Oh yes, she can!' said the kingfisher. 'I get what

she's writing. I do . . . It's about Josie herself. Gaily blooming means dying.'

'It doesn't,' said the buffalo.

'I've never gaily bloomed,' said the kingfisher, 'and I'm alive.'

'Are you?' asked the hedgehog.

'Yes,' said the kingfisher. 'I'm alive. Otherwise I couldn't cry, could I? *I*'ve never borne fruit in the summer.'

'Perhaps you've never really tried,' said the snowy owl. Now he was blushing right under his tail.

'What about the warm feet, then?' demanded the kingfisher. 'She writes that she has warm feet, doesn't she? Warm feet means death and cold feet means you're alive – otherwise you can't feel that you've got cold feet.'

'For goodness sake hold your tongue for once,' said the buffalo.

'Do what the boss says!' smirked the hedgehog. 'Rule one.'

Times had changed since Josie left us.

'And then she also writes . . .' said the kingfisher.

'Exactly!' said the desert fox. 'She writes! So she can't be dead, can she?'

'It's *me* that's not dead,' said the kingfisher, 'because I've never yet laughed in the winter.'

'You've been alive a long time,' said the hedgehog.

'I have.'

'You've lived so long by now,' said the hedgehog, and he looked at the kingfisher with eyes like scythes, which sliced from his grey crest to the wrinkles on his toes and back again, 'if you would like to be dead for a bit, you can clear off.'

'Cut it out now!' cried the buffalo. 'Let's keep it friendly, if you please!'

'Yes,' said the kingfisher. 'No rows! The fact that Josie is dead is bad enough . . . I can't die because I've got to keep look-out – rule four.'

'Go and do it, then!' cried the hedgehog.

The kingfisher put on his hat, pulled his scarf round him and strode out of the door with dignity, to his place on the quay.

And that was how it happened that the kingfisher was the first to see the swan.

Like a great white ship she came into the little harbour. On her back sat a baby. It was a pretty picture, the naked child on the ship of white feathers. The child had its arms round the swan's neck and sat warmly between the great wings.

We ran out of the inn to the quay. We made encouraging noises, but the swan came no closer. She drifted in the middle of the harbour. Quite silently. The baby cried.

We ran to our houses and came back with bread and sponge fingers, rusks and bananas. The buffalo brought a bottle of milk. We stood in a row on the quay and made our encouraging noises, but the swan came no closer.

The buffalo flung the bottle in a great arc into the water, just by the swan. We did the same.

You could see that the swan knew what was good for the baby. First she swam to the bread, then to the bottle of milk and one banana. The rest she ate herself. When there was nothing left, the baby released the swan's neck and tumbled over backwards among the feathers. The swan laid her beak against the baby's cheek.

We whispered quietly, the sea rocked the harbour, the baby and the swan fell asleep.

Every day we threw milk and bread and bananas to the baby, and rusks and sponge fingers to the swan. Every day the baby grew fatter. The swan lay deeper and deeper in the water. But she came no closer to the quay.

The baby thought it was all wonderful. The water was already above its navel, but it splashed the water with little flat hands and crowed and trampled, and look . . . the trampling helped!

One day the swan was lying so still and deep in the water that she could no longer move. We held our breath.

But . . . the baby trampled with its little legs and made its hands into oars. It pulled them through the water: one by one, from front to back, left right, left right, and so . . . they moved slowly forwards. The baby steered the swan to the quay.

There are steps there, stone steps, from the bottom of the harbour to the high quay. The baby steered the swan to the steps. The swan's breast came to rest on a step that was just under the water. The child set its feet on the step, left right, beside the swan, and stood up.

It stood up!

'Bless my soul!' said the kingfisher. 'Another little girl.'

'Naturally,' said the buffalo, 'little girls make the world go round.'

'And boys?'

'Boys make sure that girls always keep on doing it,' said the buffalo.

The little girl walked up the steps. She walked! With legs bowed from sitting on the swan all the time, but she walked. She climbed! The buffalo took her in his arms and walked off the quay, away from the harbour. The little girl did not look round.

The swan shook her feathers loose and swam into the harbour, away from the steps; out of the harbour,

away from the child. She did not look round. But when she was travelling on the sea like a great white ship, she stretched out her neck. She opened her wings, rose towards the sky and sang.

She flew towards the light that shone through the blue sky, and higher, where she lost her wings, and higher, where she lost her body. All that was left was her song.

And the blue turned to pink and through the pink the song rang white as a swan.